Silver Dolphin Books
An imprint of Printers Row Publishing Group
A division of Readerlink Distribution Services, LLC
10350 Barnes Canyon Road, Suite 100, San Diego, CA 92121
www.silverdolphinbooks.com

Printers Row Publishing Group is a division of Readerlink Distribution
Services, LLC.
Silver Dolphin Books is a registered trademark of Readerlink Distribution Services, LLC.

All notations of errors or omissions should be addressed to
Silver Dolphin Books,
Editorial Department, at the above address. All other correspondence
(author inquiries, permissions) concerning the content of this book should be
addressed to:
Elephant & Bird Books
201, Parkway House, Sheen Lane
London SW14 8LS. U.K.

ISBN: 978-1-68412-648-4
Manufactured, printed, and assembled in Heshan, China.
First printing, December 2018. LP/12/18.
22 21 20 19 18   1 2 3 4 5

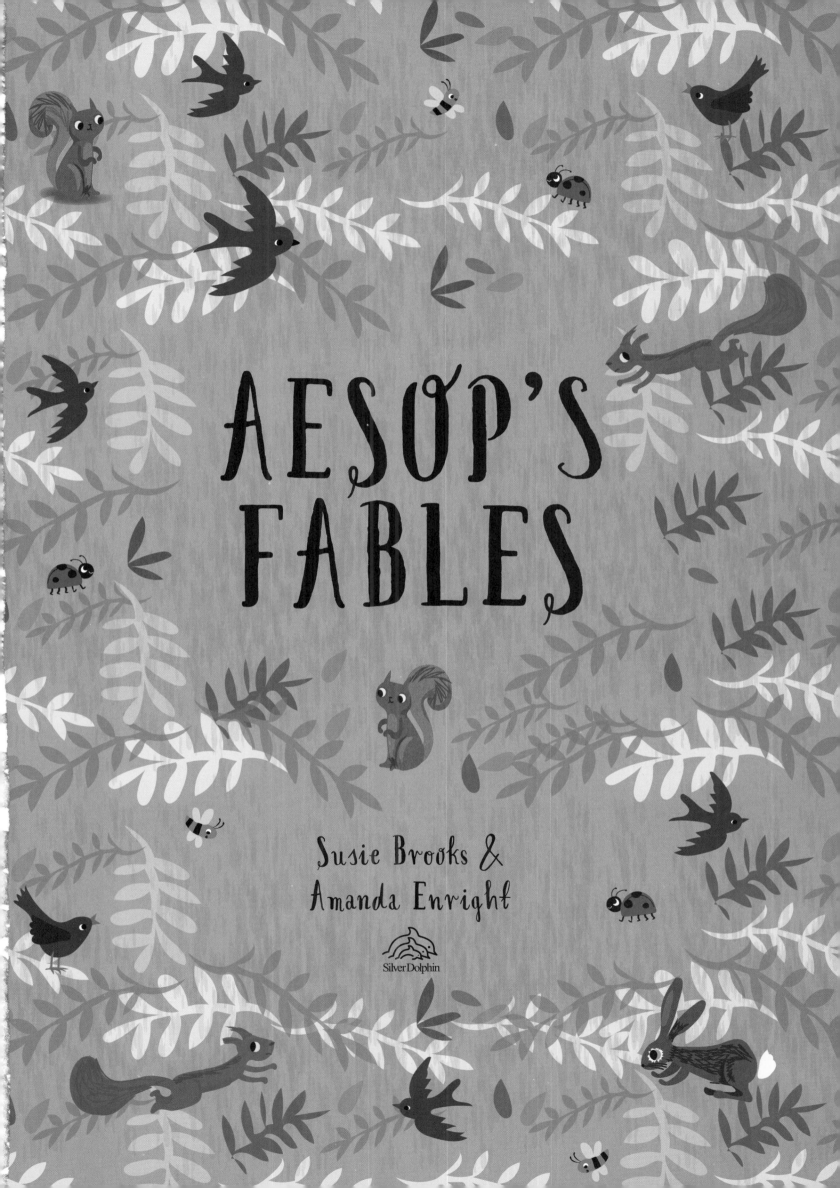

AESOP'S FABLES

Susie Brooks &
Amanda Enright

Silver Dolphin

Contents

The Tortoise and the Hare

Tortoise was never in a hurry for anything. Ever.
Even on his birthday, he would open his presents v-e-r-y
s-l-o-w-l-y, so it was nearly his next birthday by the time
he'd finished. Tortoise's friend Squirrel got so bored watching
that she decided not to wrap things anymore.

One particular morning, Tortoise was s-t-r-o-l-l-i-n-g
in the sunshine, munching on a fallen leaf and thinking it must
soon be time for a long winter's sleep.

CHOMP · CHOMP · CHOMP...

He chewed every mouthful fifty times while he daydreamed
about fluffy feather pillows.

Tortoise was just wondering if Bird
could help him make a duvet when...
WHOOOSH! A huge, fast blast
of air whistled right past
his sleepy little nose...

"Catch me if you can!" bellowed bouncy Hare, who was showing off to a bunch of buzzing bees. "Look how fast I can run!" And Hare roared off around the woodland, up a high hill, and back again before Tortoise could blink.

Hare wasn't even out of breath. He carried on bouncing and bellowing, "Come on slow-pokes, keep up! Don't you all wish you were as speedy as me?"

The bees and butterflies all nodded, "It would be wonderful to be that quick." But Tortoise just gazed quietly up at Hare's whirring whiskers and muttered, "No."

Hare was so busy hopping, his flapping ears didn't hear the answer. "Who wants to race me?" he babbled on.

There was a l-o-n-g, s-l-o-w silence.

Then Tortoise answered, louder this time, "I will!"

Hare nearly fell over in shock.
"YOU? A s-1-o-w, plodding
Tortoise, want to race ME?"

HEEE HEEEE
HEEEEEE

"Why not?" replied Tortoise. "Scared I might beat you?"

Hare was quivering now, not because he was the teeniest bit scared but because his sides were almost splitting with giggles. "YOU, beat ME? But you're the slowest animal in the whole wide world!"

"Let's see then," yawned Tortoise, staring straight into Hare's glistening eyes. "There's no rush. I'll meet you at the start line next week."

Tortoise thought he should probably do some training. He attempted a push-up, but his shell was rather heavy.

When he rolled over for a sit-up, the ants had to help him get back up!

Tortoise s-t-r-e-t-c-h-e-d his legs and held his head high...

Then he nibbled a four-leafed clover and
set off v-e-r-y s-l-o-w-l-y
for the start line.

"Do you think he'll make it?" whispered Bird.

"Hard to tell," said Squirrel. "I'm not sure if he's moving yet."

Hare was just around the corner chatting with Fox. He was blabbering nonstop as usual—something about tails and why a short, white fluffy one was far better for sprinting than a big orange brush. When Tortoise trundled into sight, Hare let out a snicker and a snort.

"Hey Fox, have you ever heard anything so funny? That dozy dawdler thinks he can beat me in a race!"

Fox looked from Hare to Tortoise and back again with a grin.

"I tell you what, I'll start the race for you!" he cried.

Hare and Tortoise were delighted.
Sharp-eyed Fox wouldn't allow any cheating.
They shook paws politely and said, "See you next week."

On the day of the race, an excited crowd gathered at the start line. Tortoise, who had taken all week to walk there, was sitting and thinking about tomorrow's breakfast. He was very happy to be kept waiting by Hare, who arrived not a second too early or late with a noisy,

'YEEEEEE-HAH!"

Hare took his position next to Tortoise and chanted, "Morning Mr. Slow-Poke. I hope you're in the mood to LOSE!" Tortoise shrunk into his shell to block out the noise. "First one to touch the tree over the hill—and NO cheating," Fox began explaining the rules. Then he screamed,

"On your marks, get set... GO!"

and blew a shrill whistle.

Faster than a sneeze, Hare was leaping and bounding and **WHOOPING** into the distance. Tortoise, still a tiny bit distracted by his breakfast plans, inched s-l-o-w-l-y forwards over the start line. "At least I can enjoy the race in peace now," he thought, as he watched the white, fluffy tail disappear in a blur.

The birds and bees
were busy making bets on
the winner. It was very clear to
all of them that Hare would be the
champion, and by more than a
whisker too. "Come on, Tortoise!" called Snail,
who was determined that his s-l-o-w,
shelled friend had a chance.

"WHOOOP! COME ON, TORTOISE!"

A familiar bellow came out of the blue. It was Hare, back again, having sprinted a whole lap of the first field, "Didn't you hear the whistle? It's time to START!"

"I have started," said Tortoise with a sigh. And with that, Hare groaned and sped off in the opposite direction.

Very soon, Hare decided there wasn't much point in running. He could win this race blindfolded, hopping on one leg or even standing on his head. So he slumped down by a tree to enjoy the sunshine.

"This is the life," thought Hare, "I've got all the time in the world." And he fell asleep.

Meanwhile, Tortoise just p-l-o-d-d-e-d slowly on. It really was a lovely day for plodding, and he had plenty of friends to keep him company. He wondered how Hare ever enjoyed anything when he hurtled everywhere at such a silly speed. "I bet he's got some blisters or a cramp in the stomach by now," Tortoise thought.

The bright, sunny day s-l-o-w-l-y faded into evening. Fox was waiting by the finish line and listening out for the thundering of Hare's feet. "He must be here soon," Fox said to Squirrel.

Then Fox glimpsed
something moving very
s-t-e-a-d-i-l-y in the distance.

It was Tortoise!

Fox couldn't believe his eyes. Tortoise plodded c-l-o-s-e-r and c-l-o-s-e-r, step by step... until it looked like he was actually going to **WIN!**

Tortoise was simply thinking how much nearer he was to tomorrow's breakfast. "An extra clump of dandelions and some alfalfa, **YUM**..." Then he blinked for a moment and glanced around. He couldn't see Hare!

"WHERE IS HARE?" Tortoise cried, slightly startled.

The animals all looked at each other...

"WHERE ON EARTH IS HARE?"

Well Hare was still snoring away by the tree near the start!

He was dreaming about being crowned the winner, **THE FASTEST ANIMAL IN THE LAND**. Hare lifted the trophy, took a deep bow, and with a mighty **CHEER** from the **ROARING** crowd...

"**THE RACE!**" he yelped, leaping to his feet and almost tripping over his droopy whiskers. "How long have I been asleep for? **HELP!** Does anybody know?"

Quick as a flash, Hare sprinted off again. He wasn't **WHOOPING** this time.

Hare HURRIED and he SCURRIED and he rushed
and he raced, so quickly that the wind whistled in
his ears. He ran and he RAN, fast as his legs would carry
him, until he caught sight of the tree over the hill.

Could it be...?

Could it POSSIBLY be Tortoise?

Is that TORTOISE c-r-e-e-p-i-n-g over the finish line?

The crowd cheered for real this time. It WAS Tortoise,
and over all his friends' roars he could hear Hare's
thundering paws!

Tortoise touched the winning tree just as Hare was screeching up behind him.

"It's not fair," Hare panted, "I fell asleep!"

He was NOT in the mood to lose.

"Tortoise won fair and square," replied Fox, "No cheating!" And he winked at Tortoise, who was considering eating the bark off the winning tree trunk.

V-e-r-y s-l-o-w-l-y, Tortoise turned to Hare and offered to share tomorrow's breakfast.

"Thanks, Mr. Slow-Poke." Hare heard himself say, "You'd better start now or I'll finish all the dandelions before you."

"We'll see," replied Tortoise, with a s-l-o-w smile.

The Moral for  The Tortoise and the Hare:

Slow and
steady wins
the race.

The Town Mouse and the Country Mouse

Town Mouse liked everyone, everywhere to know that he was **INCREDIBLY** grand.

He slept in a bed with the softest bedding, wore fine tailored clothes, and strutted about the streets in a fancy hat, with his long, whiskered nose in the air.

There was very little that Town Mouse didn't have— but he still needed porters to carry his shopping bags!

His latest purchase was a small silver cheese knife, which showed his reflection beautifully. Town Mouse loved cheese, but only the expensive kind that arrived in a paper wrapper from the delicatessen down the road.

One morning, Town Mouse received an invitation.
It came from his cousin, Country Mouse.

Town Mouse was fond of Country Mouse, though they lived
very different lives. He decided to accept and pay his dear
cousin a visit.

"Dear Cousin Country Mouse,

Thank you for your invitation.
I shall be arriving on the
afternoon train.
Kindly send your driver to collect me."

Town Mouse spent a long time dressing for his trip to the country.

He had eaten too much cheese for his favorite trousers...

He might catch a chill in his exquisite silk shirt...

"All that country mud!" he winced, as he took off his stylish shoes.

Finally, he settled for his best tweed waistcoat and red velvet bow tie.

"My, how handsome I look!"

Meanwhile, in the middle of what Town Mouse called "Nowhere," Country Mouse was getting ready for her visitor.

She swept, and she scrubbed, and she plumped up her straw-stuffed cushions...

She asked the spiders to please move their webs somewhere else.

She collected corn from the fields and leaves from the garden.

"Oh he's going to LOVE my new recipe!" she sang.

Country Mouse spent the whole afternoon at her smoky hot stove, gnawing the leaves from nettles and boiling them in fresh puddle water. An unlucky ant plopped into the saucepan. "Ooh yummy!" she thought.

There was some bread in the cupboard—a little old but good for the teeth. And what could they have for dessert?

"That's easy," laughed Country Mouse, "Cheesecake!" She had a wonderful way of crushing cookies for the base—by stuffing them into her socks and stomping on them.

The next day, Town Mouse arrived as promised on the afternoon train. He waited a while, but no driver appeared, so he huffed and puffed and teetered across the fields to Country Mouse's house.

It was quite a journey, and more than twice Town Mouse fell flat on his snooty nose and had to clean the mud from his whiskers. A kind bird pecked the twigs from his hat and offered him a worm to keep him going.

Town Mouse had to admit that he was hungry, and he hoped very much that a fine and fancy cheese board would be waiting for him at Country Mouse's house.

Finally, limping a little from a stone in his boot, he arrived.

Well, Country Mouse lived in a tree stump.
It was **NOT** what Town Mouse was used to.

"Good day, dear Cousin! Er no, I won't sit down just yet."

Country Mouse threw open her arms to hug her guest (she was
still a bit sticky from cooking). "Would you like a cup of bramble
tea?" she squeaked.

Town Mouse politely replied that he'd rather have something more substantial, so Country Mouse laid the table for lunch. "It's my best nettle soup and corn mash!" she squealed excitedly, "Please tell me—what do you think?"

Town Mouse looked at Country Mouse and then looked around her house. It didn't take long, because the tree stump was particularly small. The walls were damp and the straw-stuffed cushions were scratchy. He wondered if Country Mouse ever vacuumed her old moss rug.

Town Mouse was perched on the edge of a wobbly stool, with ants perilously close to his bottom.

"I think, dear Cousin, you live too simply. You should come with me to the city!"

So Town Mouse went on to talk about his soft bedding and his tailors and his porters and his fancy cheese...while nibbling crumbs of dry barley bread and wishing he could have some butter. The cheesecake could have been worse, he thought, though it had a strange aftertaste of feet.

Country Mouse sat on her dusty toadstool and listened. It did all sound **INCREDIBLY** grand! She had never been to the city before, and she could save up to buy some new socks.

"I'd love to come with you, dear Cousin, if you'll have me!" "It's settled then," he replied, brushing a pesky ant from his sleeve.

That night, snuggled up in her warm leafy nest, Country Mouse dreamt of all the riches that Town Mouse had told her about. She couldn't wait to go and visit! Her best dress was slightly torn around the edges, but she would ask a friendly spider to spin some new threads.

Country Mouse got up early to pack—so early that an owl swooped in to ask what she was doing! As soon as he heard she was going to the city, he lent her a beautiful feather for her hat.

Meanwhile, Town Mouse found the nest terribly prickly and woke up in a bad mood. He refused the leftover barley bread for breakfast, and sipped on a cup of bitter bramble tea.

"Are you ready yet, Country Mouse?"

he bellowed.

He had never been so glad to be going home.

So the two mice set off for the city. This time, Town Mouse had sent for his driver and a porter to carry his luggage. Country Mouse squealed with delight at the sight of the magnificent red car! As they chugged along the bumpy country roads, Town Mouse got the feeling that some ants might be traveling in his underwear.

"You were **NOT** invited," he scowled.

When Country Mouse arrived at Town Mouse's mansion, the door looked utterly HUGE!

Everything inside the house was SHINY!

Country Mouse bounced on the sofas and slid down the bannisters and dipped her toes in bubbling champagne...

WHEEEEEEEE! The chandelier jingled as she swung by her tail and flew off onto a lavish rug.

The two merry mice were just looting the cupboard when...
WOOOOOF. A big, booming BARK startled
Country Mouse right out of her new city socks!

"What's that?" she trembled, darting into a sugar bowl and
rattling its silver spoon.

"It's the dogs... Follow me!"

And Town Mouse disappeared...

WOOOOOOOOOOOF!

Country Mouse chased her cousin, quick as she could across the soft, squishy carpet...

Under an antique armchair...

Over two velvet slippers...

Behind a brass-handled cabinet...

And into a hole.

WOOOOOOOOOOOF!

It was dark in the hole. And chilly. The big, booming
WOOOOF was soon joined by a screeching
MEOOWW.

Country Mouse shuddered and dreamt of her cozy tree stump,
her leafy nest, and all the quiet hiding places in her garden.

"I want to go home," she whimpered.

Later that night, the house fell silent and the two mice crept out of their hole.

"I've had enough of your luxury life," squeaked Country Mouse. "I'm going back to my nice, safe tree stump!"

"Very well," sighed Town Mouse. And he scuttled off to find some truffles and a fresh cotton wool ball for his pillow.

LA-DE-DA...

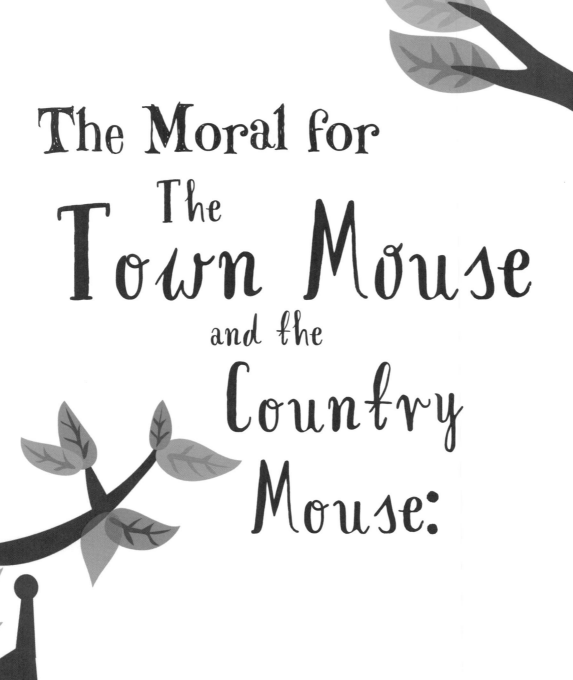

The Moral for
The
Town Mouse
and the
Country
Mouse:

There's
no place
like home.

The Frog and the Ox

It was a brand new day for a nearly new Frog, and Frog was very excited. She was going on an adventure, ON HER OWN, away from her 107 brothers and sisters. Frog (who didn't have a name because her parents couldn't think of that many) had wanted to be an explorer ever since she was a teeny tadpole. She wondered what she would see in the big, wide world, and if she would meet anyone but frogs.

BOING!

Frog knew that no one would notice if she hopped away from home—her mom and dad weren't good at counting, and anyway 108 frog children made **A LOT** of noise. So she popped out of her damp hollow and into the sunshine, swiveling her googly eyes all around her.

Frog hopped and hopped, further than she had ever been, leaping the long grass and flicking out her tongue to catch flies. Soon she came to a pond that was much, much bigger than the one her mom made her have a bath in.

"Hooray, I need a swim!" Frog thought, and she prepared to take a leap into the water.
But just as she was flexing her toes to dive in, she let out a loud,

"Riiibitt!"

Standing in the pond,
Frog saw a MONSTER.

58

It really was a monster, with a huge spiky head, a swishing tail, and hard feet that flew in her direction. A throaty "ooooooRRRRRR" was booming from its snout, and its shaggy ears were flapping in the breeze.

Frog hopped around the front end to get a better look, launching herself from a lily pad.

BOING!

BOING!

BOING!

She simply couldn't jump that high!
Brother 23 had told her stories about
monsters, but she had never imagined they would
be this huge. Her wide mouth dropped open with a tremble.

"H-hello?" she croaked, hopping
dangerously close to a hairy knee.
"E-excuse me, but what are you?
And d-do you have a name?"

The monster just stared
from beneath a furry fringe,
stuck out its tongue, and said,

"OOOOOOORRRRRRR."

Frog nearly jumped
out of her skin.

Frog had to tell someone about the gigantic, bellowing monster that was paddling in the far-off pond! She didn't really know anyone other than her family, so she hopped and hopped all the way back home.

"DAD!" she screamed, in a voice that was higher than normal. "DAAAAD, guess what—I met a MONSTER!"

Frog's dad was gobbling his breakfast—a big pile of worms and slugs that slipped down nicely without any chewing. He was not entirely pleased to be interrupted by whichever of his children this was.

"QUIET!" he roared, but Frog carried on, speaking so quickly that she twisted her long tongue. "It was the biggest creature I've ever seen, with a spiky head and hard feet and shaggy ears and hairy knees and it made a loud noise like this...

"oooOOOORRRRRRR."

Frog's dad harrumphed.

"Was it as big as me?" he asked
after a while, patting his big belly as he slurped down his
very last slug. Frog's dad was a very proud bullfrog. He had
spent many years just eating and sitting and hopping as little
as possible to improve the size of his waist.

"WAY bigger than you!" squealed Frog, and she sprang up
into the air to try and show how tall the monster was.

"You do too much exercise," Frog's dad grunted, "No wonder you're so teeny. Anyone would seem like a giant to you!"

But Frog wailed in protest, "Honestly Dad, the monster could have swallowed you, me, and all my 107 brothers and sisters whole!"

Frog's dad belched. As far as he was concerned, there was no such thing as a monster. And he knew from his own reflection in the pond that HE was the largest creature in the land.

Frog decided there was only one thing to do. She would have to take her dad to see the monster.

She tugged at his flabby elbow, "Come on Dad, let's GO!" The bullfrog's flesh wobbled, but he didn't budge an inch. Next, Frog took a running hop and pushed at her dad from behind, but still he wouldn't move—Frog just bounced back and landed face first in the water.

"PLEASE Dad," Frog spluttered, wiping a muddy twig from her mouth. "You have to see it to believe it. Everyone should meet at least one monster in their lifetime!"

"Fine," sighed the bullfrog eventually. "But only to prove that no monster is bigger than me."

So Frog's dad heaved his bulbous belly and tried to hop.
He tried to hop, but... FLOP.
Hop... FLOP. Hop... FLOP.
His belly was too heavy and full of slugs!

Frog's dad was soon so out of breath that he took in a very deep inhale. And then something extraordinary happened. His belly swelled up to twice its normal size, just like a balloon!

"Was the monster **THIS** big?" he gasped.

Frog fell over in amazement.

"Bigger!
BIGGER!" she screeched.

Frog's dad would not be defeated. He gulped again—a huge
gulp of air that made him bulge even more, like a beach ball.

"THIS big?"

"Bigger!" squealed Frog.

"THIS big?"

"Bigger!"

"THIS big?"

By now Frog's dad was quite enjoying the challenge.
An excited crowd had gathered round, and Frog's 107
brothers and sisters were waving their arms and legs like
cheerleaders. Frog's mom, on the other hand, was tutting
disapprovingly from a distance, worried she would have to
measure him for a new coat.

Meanwhile, back at the pond, the monster was minding its own business and going "OOOOOOOOORRRRR."
He thought about the little green bouncy thing on the lily pad and said, "Couldn't she tell I'm just a harmless Ox?"

You see the Ox was really a kind soul, but he did enjoy a joke. So he decided to go in search of the little green bouncy thing and make her jump once more.

With a loud splash, the Ox heaved himself out of the water and stumbled ashore. He shook his hairy coat so hard that all the trees around him got a sprinkling. Then he took a few chomps from the long, wet grass and plodded on his way. "Little green bouncy things live in little damp hollows," he thought. "I know just where to find one of them.

"OOOOOORRRRRRRR."

The Ox had a nice stroll into the woods. He said "OOOORRRRRRR" to a squirrel and chuckled as its tail hair stood on end. "ooooooORRRRRRR." he boomed again and a whole family of birds flapped right out of their nest! He was just creeping up behind a particularly sleepy rabbit when a loud commotion came from the bushes.

"Howzabout THIS?" the Ox heard. The voice sounded very squeaky and strange.

"Much BIGGER!" heard the Ox.

"This big?"

"BIGGER!"

At this point there was an unusual silence,
followed by 109 small gulps of air.
The Ox held his breath and listened.
All of a sudden, there came a gigantic...

POP!

Frog came bouncing into the clearing and didn't even blink at the monster this time. "I think Dad got too big for his boots," she said.

And what do you think the monster Ox replied?

"OOOOOOOOOOORRRRRRR."

The Moral for The Frog and the Ox:

Being too big-headed can lead to trouble.

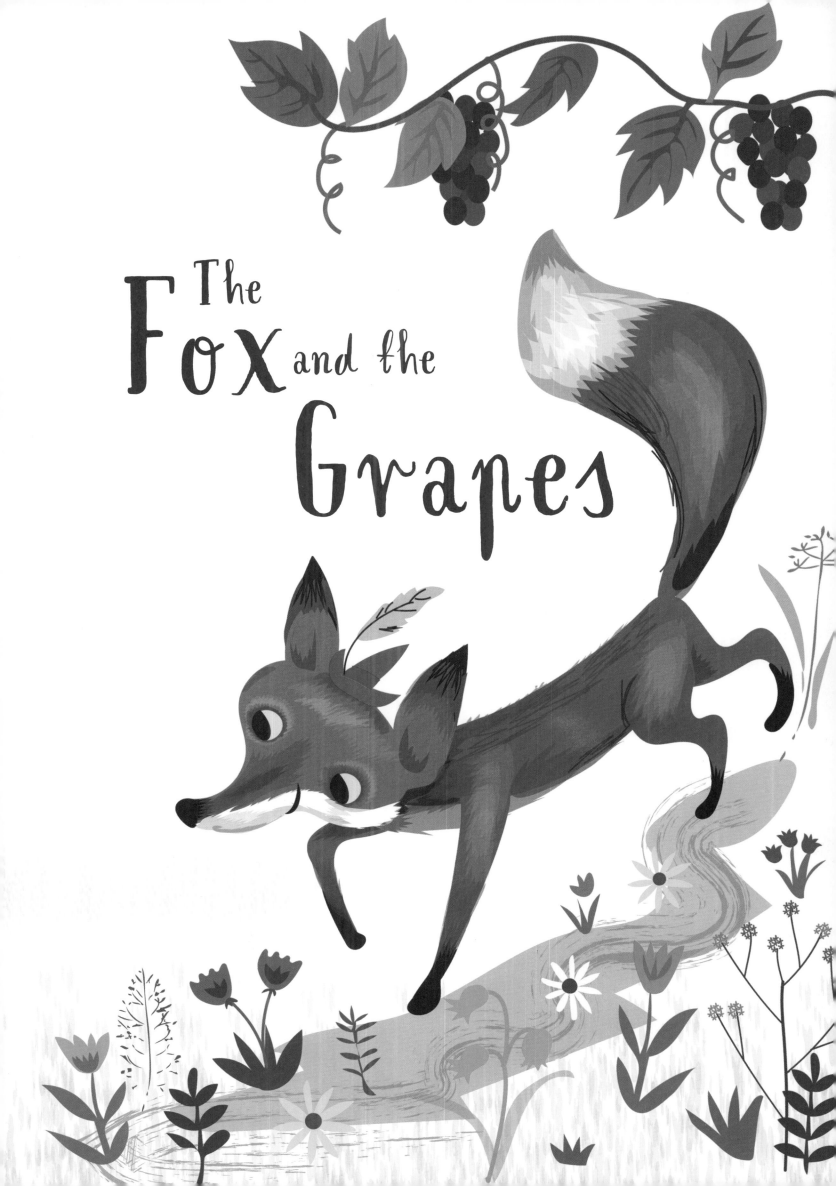

The Fox and the Grapes

Fox was very good at getting his own way—
after all, it's what foxes do best. He was just
licking his lips after a particularly tasty
chicken bone, when...

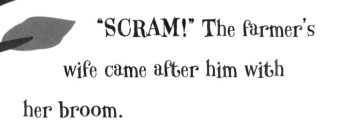

"SCRAM!" The farmer's wife came after him with her broom.

Well, we all know you can't run in slippers, as the farmer's wife quickly found out...

No sooner had she fallen—SPLAT!—on her red face... when Fox leapt over her head, snatched the sausage roll from her hand, and dived deftly through a gap in the bushes.

HA!

Fox stopped to check his reflection in the mirror of a muddy old tractor.

"Not a whisker out of place. Marvelous!"

Fox decided that a nice plump duck was just what he wanted for his main course. So he trotted off on his toes with his pointed ears listening for QUACKS.

BBBBRRRRRRM

That wasn't a QUACK. The muddy old tractor was rumbling fast toward him with an angry-looking farmer at the wheel...

BBBBRRRRRRRRM

Quick as a flash, Fox somersaulted into a ditch, whipping his white-tipped tail in just in time.

HA!

Fox picked himself up, brushed himself off, and checked his reflection in a puddle.

"Not a whisker out of place. Marvelous!"

And he tiptoed into the woods.

There were lots of SWISHING leaves in the woods.
And lots of CRACKING twigs. A frog CROAKED and
an owl HOOTED... But Fox couldn't hear any QUACKS.

He kept on tiptoeing through the trees, snacking on a worm
along the way.

Soon he began to feel thirsty. "I wish I'd had had a drink
from that puddle," he thought.

Just then, up high, out of the corner of
Fox's eye...

HA! He saw a very juicy bunch of grapes.

Fox stared up at the grapes, drooling and dreaming of
all the delicious, thirst-quenching juice inside.
They were much too high for him to reach.

"Not a problem for a clever guy like me!" Fox grinned.

And then he LEAPED.

To be fair, it wasn't a bad leap, but Fox didn't even come close. Next he took a run-up... LEAP!

It was good but not good enough.

He ran and jumped again...

MISSED!

He sprinted and sprang again...

MISSED!

Again...

MISSED!

And again...

MISSED!

Fox LEAPT and JUMPED and BOUNDED and BOUNCED...

But still the grapes stayed on the vine.

At last Fox took his biggest leap yet and... he
SOMERSAULTED! He tumbled through the air,
over and over, landing in a ball and rolling down, downhill
away from the grapes. THUMP.

Fox looked over at the grapes with a snarl. "I bet they're
not really that juicy," he sighed.
"And I know they'd taste horribly sour.
I didn't want grapes for dinner anyway. Or ducks. YUCK."

And with that, he loped off sulkily, back to his den, not
even listening for QUACKS.

The Moral for The Fox and the Grapes:

It is easy to
hate what you
can't have.

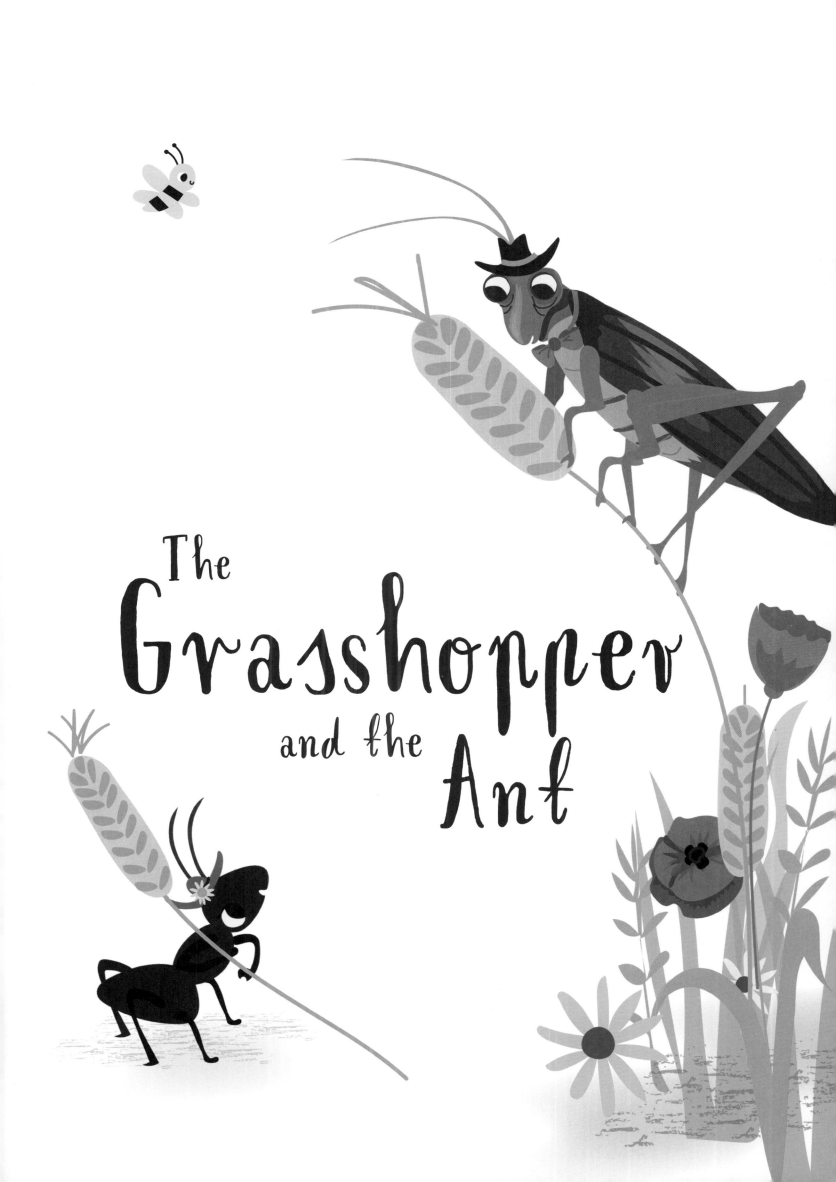

The Grasshopper
and the
Ant

It was a glorious summer's day—the kind of day that Grasshopper liked to spend sitting and eating and doing not very much hopping at all.

He was fluttering through the farm searching for breakfast, when...

"ZING!" A huge flash of gleaming gold suddenly dazzled his big, bulging eyes.

Grasshopper blinked and then jumped for joy (almost energetically). There in front of him was a giant cornfield— and it just so happened that corn was his favorite food in the whole, wide world. Grasshopper sat in his cornfield and ate, thinking how lucky he was that none of his greedy relatives were there to share it with him.

"This is the life!" chirped Grasshopper, lounging lazily on a leaf. "I will eat and eat corn for FOREVER!"

Soon Grasshopper was so happy with his corn-filled tummy that he started to sing. Well, he called it singing but really he was scraping his leg against his scratchy wing and making noise.

"Hey, Ant!" called Grasshopper, "Do you like my latest tune?"

TRRRRRR. TRRRRRRR. TRRRRRRR.

Ant was busy trying not to trip as she carried a heavy ear of corn. "I can't stop to listen to your music," she puffed, "I've got too much work to do!"

"Work?" snickered Grasshopper, "What a waste of time on a beautiful sunny day like today!" And he lay back to play another verse while a fluttering poppy fanned his face.

TRRRRRR. TRRRRRRR. TRRRRRRR.

TRRRRRR. TRRRRRRR. TRRRRRRR.

Grasshopper sang and the poppy fluttered and Ant
just kept on marching...

Left...

Right...

To...
Fro...

Grasshopper felt exhausted watching her!

"Where are you taking all that corn, silly Ant?"

"To my nest, to store it for winter."

Grasshopper saw
no sense in storing,
when he had all the corn
he wanted right here.
"Silly Ant," he huffed again, loud enough for her to hear.

So Grasshopper carried on sitting... and eating... and snoozing... and singing... until Snail moaned he couldn't get any sleep.

"PLEASE, Grasshopper, turn your tunes down—I can hear you even when I hide inside my shell!"

Happily for Snail, Grasshopper had eaten himself into an excellent mood. Ready to stretch his legs a little, he agreed to hop away to a nearby meadow. There were feasts of lush green grass there, as far as his eyes could see.

"This really IS the life!" Grasshopper chirped.

But slowly the seasons began to change.

Autumn flew by in a flurry of falling leaves—
they were fun to munch on for a while!
Then farmers with huge machines came to chop down
the fields of corn, and Grasshopper caught a chill singing
in the rain. He snuffled and coughed his way into winter, as
the weather turned icy cold. Sitting still was no fun
anymore, and Grasshopper's singing wings froze.

"I'm HUNGRY!" he wailed as he stared at his old cornfield,
buried under a thick blanket of snow.

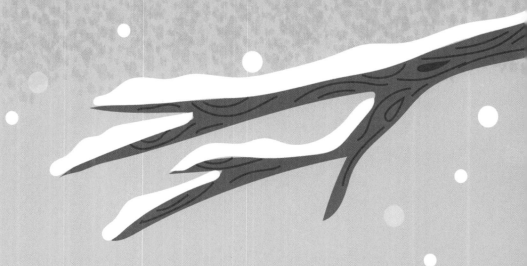

Grasshopper searched the meadows, but they were covered in snow too. He dug and he scratched and he rummaged, but he just couldn't find any food. He started to sulk.

CHoMP.

Right at that moment, a muffled munching sound tickled Grasshopper's ears...

"ANT!"

Ant heard a yell from inside her nest, where she was having a feast with her friends. She peeped outside and spotted Grasshopper, looking somewhat sorry for himself.

"Brrr, it's c-c-cold, isn't it?" he croaked, "And I can't find anything to eat."

"That's bad luck," said Ant, "We have all the food we need to get us through until spring!"

Grasshopper's mouth watered so much that an icicle formed on his chin. "Look, could you spare an ear of corn please, Ant? I didn't store any for myself."

"That serves you right for being lazy all summer," said Ant, "AND for calling me silly. Look who's the silly one now!"

And with that, Ant left Grasshopper's tummy to rumble and scuttled back to her feast.

Munch, munch, munch,

Burrrp.

Shiver. Rumble. Grumble.

The Moral for The Grasshopper and the Ant:

A bit of hard
work now
will pay off
later.

The Lion and the Mouse

In a very tiny nest in a deep, dark jungle, there lived an adventurous little Mouse. She decided one day that she'd like to join the circus and was practicing her no-paw somersaults.

TA-DA!

It was going quite well actually. She was almost ready to try doing it backwards when...

RUMBLE, WHOOSH, RUMBLE, WHOOSH...
the trees started trembling and the sky started shaking
at the sound of an UPROARIOUS SNORE!
Mouse didn't know it was a snore, of course.
To her it could have been thunder or an
earthquake or even a great fire-breathing dragon.

So being the curious creature that she was, she cartwheeled
off to see where the noise was coming from.

Mouse cartwheeled and cartwheeled until she was a bit giddy. "Squeeeak!" she cried, twitching a little as the rumbling became a deafening boom. Before Mouse knew it, she was hopping rather unsteadily in front of...

a **HUMONGOUS LION's** nose.

"Squeeeeeeeek!" cried Mouse again.
"You're so BIG and your teeth are
so TALL, you could gobble me up in one nibble!"
But Lion did not hear her — he was too busy
sleeping and dreaming of making mouse sandwiches.

Mouse stood for a second to consider her options... Should she run away? Where could she hide? Would he wake up if she moved a whisker?

Then suddenly a bite-sized part of Mouse had a bite-sized but brave thought. "Wouldn't it be fun to slide down Lion's silky snout and swing in his magnificent mane!"

"HEE, HEE, HEE, lazy Lion!" she shrieked, to check that he was still asleep. "You're dreaming of eating mice like me, aren't you? Well here I am, come and get me!"

The lazy Lion did not move—he didn't even blink. So little Mouse took a giant leap backwards...

WHEEEEEEEEEE!

Mouse landed on Lion's hairy brow and gulped—she wasn't scared of heights, but a real live Lion was a lot more dangerous than a trapeze. Then, with a whoop of glee, she slid down Lion's snout...

WHEEEEEE! She flew right off the end and landed with a handspring flip.

Next, she scrambled right up Lion's side...and somersaulted down his back!

"This is FUN!" she cried.

Finally, Mouse skipped to the top of Lion's magnificent mane and... **ROOOOAR.**

Just as Mouse was snatching a shiny strand to swing on...

"ROOOOAR! DO NOT MESS UP MY MAGNIFICENT MANE!"

"SQUEEEEAK." Mouse toppled over as Lion's head shook, landing right by his powerful paws. She felt her whiskers shake.

"I'm going to gobble you up in one nibble," bellowed Lion, slightly surprised to find a ready-made meal at his feet. I'll eat you with a splash of caterpillar juice and a side of dried warthog."

"I wouldn't do that if I were you," Mouse squealed.

"Why not?" enquired Lion, grabbing her by the tail.

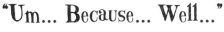

"Um... Because... Well..."

Mouse didn't really know why not—she probably would be quite tasty. So she shut her eyes tight, ready to be eaten, and hoped it would happen quickly.

There was a short pause while Lion stared at her, wondering if her tail would be good with spaghetti sauce. And then a bite-sized part of Mouse had a bite-sized but brilliant thought.
"I could come and help YOU some day," she said excitedly.

Well, the idea of a midget Mouse helping him was the funniest thing Lion had ever heard! He instantly burst out laughing, and his laugh was even louder than his snores.

Lion ROARED and GUFFAWED and he CHORTLED and he CHUCKLED... he SNORTED and he SNIGGERED until tears streamed from his eyes. The mighty beast cackled and he tittered and he howled and he snickered... and all the time he GIGGLED, little Mouse WRIGGLED.

At last, clutching his heaving belly, Lion let Mouse go.

"You're too funny to eat," he gasped, "You give me a belly ache!"

Mouse felt a tiny bit dazed and dizzy, but she wasn't taking any chances. She thanked Lion very much and scuttled away.

"I mean it!" she called over her shoulder, "Just you wait and see—I'll come to your rescue when you least expect me to!"

So Lion wandered back toward his lair, fussing about his mane and wondering where he'd left his hairbrush. His belly was still reminding him that he hadn't laughed so hard in a long time.

"A tiny mouse helping ME, HEE HEEEEEE!" Lion had to stop himself thinking about it before he burst into tears again, so he put on his serious face and strolled on through the jungle. But just as he was passing his favorite scratching tree, a loud CREEEEAK came from above and...

WHAM!
An enormous hunter's net
crashed down right on top of him!
Lion was trapped.
He felt like a helpless kitten.

Mouse was far away in the forest, rehearsing her trapeze act on a dangling vine. Who needed a mane to swing on anyway? She dangled with one hand, and then with one foot, and even looped-the-loop with her tail.

ROOOOOOAR. Just then, a muffled moan rang eerily through the trees.

ROOOOOOOOOOAAR.

"That sounds familiar," Mouse said to herself, while she timed how long she could last standing on one leg. "I wonder what it could be?"

After thirty-nine seconds, Mouse toppled over, so she cartwheeled off to see where the noise was coming from.

Well when Mouse saw who was ROARING, she just started GNAWING. Fast as her tiny teeth could go, she chewed and chewed through the net. Lion was struggling and clawing at his poor tangled mane—he really wasn't helping. Mouse gave him a nip on the nose and told him to keep still.

Nibble, nibble,
bit by bit...
it was a big job for a little
Mouse, but finally Lion
was free!

"Jumping jungles—you rescued me!" roared Lion.

"Told you so," said Mouse, "I may be little, but I can be a **BIG** help!"

Lion blinked and scooped Mouse up into his paws. For a split-second, Mouse thought she was headed for his stomach. But all Lion did was give her a big, sloppy kiss.

"Thank you," said Lion.

And from that day onward, Lion and Mouse were the best of friends.

He let her practice her circus skills. And she even braided his mane.

The Moral for
The
Lion
and the
Mouse:

If you are kind to others, they will be kind to you too.

The Fox and the Crow

"It really is quite AMAZING being me!" thought Crow,
as she sat sheltered in a tree one particularly drizzly day,
watching all the animals below look wet and gloomy.
Earlier on, Crow had swooped out for a shower, startled a
set of soggy picnickers, and won herself a very large,
very stinky piece of cheese. Oops!

No one could call Crow a picky eater, but stinky cheese was one of her favorites. She held it happily in her pointy black beak, savoring the salty, smelly, cheesy flavors and imagining its slow and slippery journey to her belly. When it got there it might well meet the wriggly worms and eggs she had for breakfast. A cheesy, wormy, eggshell-crunchy omelette— mmmm!

Crow knew there was a word for the way she was feeling. It was right on the tip of her beak, next to the cheese... "SQU..., SL..., SM...? Ah yes, I've got it—SMUG!"

Crow felt smug, and smug felt good.

So Crow sat on her branch with her cheese in her beak and had a competition with herself to see how long she could wait to eat it.

Fox was NOT enjoying the drizzle. It made his tail go frizzy and his whiskers droop, and his long satin socks were itchy with mud. He tiptoed grumpily through the forest, wishing he had four red rubber boots and a big umbrella.

"Things can only get better," sighed Fox as a raindrop dribbled down his nose. And all of a sudden, just as the drop dripped, Fox's nose smelt... cheese.

"**CHEESE?** Why on earth can I smell CHEESE in the middle of a rainy forest?"

Fox licked his lips—he did so love cheese, especially the really stinky kind. He remembered the time when he had visited the city and spent a whole night in a supermarket. Cheddar, brie, gorgonzola... every kind of cheese you could imagine, all past their use-by dates but nevertheless delicious!

Fox looked around, left and right... down and up... a-HA!

"Good day, Mrs. Crow!" he crooned in a silky voice.

"Oh Mrs. Crow, what a lovely day for a chat,"
Fox went on, blinking another raindrop from his eye.

Crow looked at him sideways—it clearly wasn't a lovely day at all.

"Why don't you come down here beside me so we can have a good chat about... well... all sorts of things. I know some excellent jokes! What did the Fox say to the...?"

Crow peered down at Fox. "He must think I hatched yesterday," she thought. "Why would I want to hear his jokes? He's after my cheese. I know foxes love cheese—but they can't climb trees! I'm going to stay right where I am and ignore him."

Fox waited. Crow didn't move a feather.

"OK, I hate to admit it but I'm a little lost," Fox tried. "Could you please come down and point me in the right direction?"

Crow snorted. First, she had no idea where Fox was going—and second, she truly didn't care. "You don't get to eat me and my dinner that easily," she thought as she took another sniff of her beak-watering cheese.

Now Fox was getting anxious. Crow was obviously not as stupid as she looked, and he sensed he was running out of time. "Mrs. Crow, please don't take this the wrong way but I can smell something utterly revolting. Could it be that cheese you have in your beak? Perhaps it is moldy—it would be terrible if it was moldy. I've eaten moldy cheese before and my belly ached for weeks and weeks..."

Fox waited for Crow to spit the cheese out, or at least caw at him to shut up. Nothing happened.

Crow did not like the sound of a bellyache, but she wasn't going to be tricked by a greedy Fox. Besides, didn't he know that some types of cheese are **MEANT** to be moldy? "This cheese is as fresh as the day," she thought, "I stole it just this morning, straight from the packet, ripe and ready for a cracker. It smells better than perfect to me—in fact, it smells good enough to eat right **NOW**."

And Crow prepared to take a gulp...

"Oh Mrs. Crow, just look at me,
I'm soaked right through to the lining of my old
fur coat. If only you would fly down here and fan me
dry with your FABULOUS feathers."

"Fabulous?" Crow cocked her head. She liked the sound of
"fabulous" and she was incredibly proud of her glossy black
feathers. Still, she didn't have a whiff of sympathy for shivering
Fox—partly because the only whiff around her was cheese.

"Mrs. Crow, your wings are so SPLENDIFEROUS
and your beak so fine..."

"Spot on," thought Crow,

"Couldn't have put it better myself."

"Your eyes sparkle like jewels in the dark night sky!"

Crow winked and nodded, "They do."

"And you hold your head like a Queen—not just beautiful,
but powerful and wise." Crow agreed completely.
She imagined herself in a tall, twinkly crown, perched on
a grand gold nest. She would dine with a delicate silver
spoon and have all the cheese she liked brought on a cushion.

"Oh how I would love to hear you sing," Fox cried,
"I bet you're the best singer of all the birds."

Well of course it was true, according to Crow. She had
squawked a solo in the Woodland Proms and caused quite
a commotion with her rapping. Fox shuffled expectantly as
she tapped her claws on the branch and tried to remember
her hit tune.

"Well never mind," Fox huffed up at Crow, after lingering
longer than he wanted to, "If you won't sing for me, I'll
just have to go and ask Nightingale. I've heard she's started
a band with Robin and Sparrow." And he started to skulk
off, looking back sneakily over his shoulder.

Crow couldn't take it. She was ready to burst—she would NOT be outdone by a bird band! She opened her beak WIDE to reach her best high note and...

PLOP! Out fell the cheese!

Fox gobbled it up in one yummy, dribbly mouthful and rubbed his delighted tummy with a damp paw. "That's enough singing, thanks!" he spluttered, "You'll ruin my after-dinner nap."

Crow felt foolish, and foolish felt bad.

"I'll never, ever be smug or vain again," she promised herself. And she stomped off to find more worms and eggs for her lunch.

The Moral for

The
Fox
and the
Crow:

Being too proud can make you look foolish.